HARRY
the Dirty Dog

D0335510

HARRY

by Gene Zion

the Dirty Dog

Pictures by Margaret Bloy Graham

RED FOX

Also by Gene Zion
illustrated by Margaret Bloy Graham

Harry by the Sea
No Roses for Harry

A Red Fox Book

Published by Random House Children's Publishers UK
61-63 Uxbridge Road, London W5 5SA,

A division of The Random House Group Ltd
London Melbourne Sydney Auckland
Johannesburg and agencies throughout the world

Text copyright © Eugene Zion 1956
Illustrations copyright © Margaret Bloy Graham 1956

39

First published in Great Britain by
The Bodley Head Children's Books, 1956
Red Fox edition 1992

This book is sold subject to the condition that it shall not, by way of trade or otherwise,
be lent, resold, hired out, or otherwise circulated without the publisher's prior
consent in any form of binding or cover other than that in which it is published
and without a similar condition including this condition being imposed
on the subsequent purchaser.

The right of Eugene Zion and Margaret Bloy Graham to be
identified as the author and illustrator of this work
has been asserted by them in accordance with the
Copyright, Designs and Patents Act, 1988.

Printed in China

THE RANDOM HOUSE GROUP Limited Reg. No. 954009

www.randomhousechildrens.co.uk

ISBN 978 0 099 97870 1

Harry was a white dog with black spots
who liked everything,
except ... having a bath.
So one day when he heard the water
running in the tub,
he took the scrubbing brush ...

and buried it in the back garden.

Then he ran away from home.

He played where they were mending the street

and got very dirty.

He played by the railway

and got even dirtier.

He played tag with other dogs

and became dirtier still.

He slid down a coal chute
and got the dirtiest of all.
In fact, he changed

from a white dog with black spots,
to a black dog with white spots.

Although there were many other things to do, Harry began to wonder if his family thought that he had <u>really</u> run away.

He felt tired and hungry too,
so without stopping on the way
he ran back home.

When Harry got to his house,
he crawled through the fence
and sat looking at the back door.

One of the family looked out and said,
"There's a strange dog in the back garden . . .
by the way, has anyone seen Harry?"

When Harry heard this, he tried very hard
to show them he was Harry. He started to do
all his old, clever tricks. He flip-flopped

and he flop-flipped.
He rolled over and played dead.

He danced and he sang.

He did these tricks over and over again
but everyone shook their heads and said,
"Oh, no, it couldn't be Harry."

Harry gave up
and walked slowly towards the gate,
but suddenly he stopped.

He ran to a corner of the garden
and started to dig furiously.
Soon he jumped away from the hole
barking short, happy barks.

He'd found the scrubbing brush!
And carrying it in his mouth,
he ran into the house.

Up the stairs he dashed,
with the family
following close behind.

He jumped into the bathtub and sat up begging,
with the scrubbing brush in his mouth,
a trick he certainly had never done before.

"This little doggie wants a bath!"
cried the little girl, and her father said,
"Why don't you and your brother give him one?"

Harry's bath was the soapiest one he'd ever had.
It worked like magic. As soon as the children
started to scrub, they began shouting,
"Mummy! Daddy! Look, look! Come quickly!"

"It's Harry! It's Harry! It's Harry!" they cried.
Harry wagged his tail and was very, very happy.
His family combed and brushed him lovingly, and
he became once again a white dog with black spots.

It was wonderful to be home.
After dinner, Harry fell asleep
in his favourite place, happily dreaming
of how much fun it had been getting dirty.
He slept so soundly,
he didn't even feel the scrubbing brush
he'd hidden under his pillow.